Lost Country

Brahms
1st
symphony in
C minor –

Otto Kempleren

Lost Country

Dan Howell

The University of Massachusetts Press

Amherst

Printed in the United States of America
LC 93-20045
ISBN 0-87023-850-7 (cloth); 851-5 (paper)
Designed by Milenda Nan Ok Lee
Set in Adobe Garamond by Keystone Typesetting, Inc.
Printed and bound by Thomson-Shore, Inc.
Library of Congress Cataloging-in-Publication Data

Howell, Dan, 1947–
Lost country / by Dan Howell.
p.   cm.
ISBN 0–87023–850–7 (cloth : alk. paper) — ISBN
0–87023–851–5 (paper : alk. paper)
I. Title.
PS3558.08978L67   1993
811'.54—dc20   93–20045
CIP
British Library Cataloguing in Publication data are available.

for the lasting

Acknowledgments

I thank the editors of the publications in which some of the poems in this book first appeared:

Audit, an earlier version of "Whatever It Gives"; *The Environment: Essence and Issues* (Pig Iron 18, Pig Iron Press), "American Chameleon" and "The Creaturely"; *The Missouri Review,* "I'm Not Confessing Anything" and "The 4A Shuffle" (as "The 4A Shuffle"); *Prairie Schooner* (by permission of the University of Nebraska Press, © 1985 University of Nebraska Press), "Denizens" and "Last Break"; *Shankpainter,* "Kinds of Bodysurfing" and "Leisure World Safeway at Night."

I'm also grateful to the Fine Arts Work Center in Provincetown for providing the time and space and support that helped me finish this book.

Contents

I. a sighting

I'm Not Confessing Anything

> "Howell, I'm not here to punish you.
> Life will do that. Life will punish you
> enough."
> —Captain Roberto Cuesta

I was insane and a criminal in 1970, or at least
the Army or rather its doctors labeled me very
—even psychotically—depressed (although Dr.
Cuesta never fell for that really, remaining
skeptical, always smart and reliably humane
despite overwork and a hatred of "hippies,
Communists, and Socialists," and losing a fat
annual practice in Havana, in a country
also lost, no longer his), which is
exactly what I wanted the Army to think.
To be judged very sick was best after
being AWOL for 15 months (including
pursuit by the FBI—routine leg-work,
half-hearted, but the agents did manage
to come close, to locate my scattered
friends and hassle my family, including
my mother, who lived alone) and then
surrendering myself at Fort Knox,
dreading the stockade and consequently
that evening letting out tears, sobs
in front of a clerk who was hoping
to pry out some AWOL details—who
harbored me, e.g.—but succeeded
only in being a gullible audience,
my fortunate sadness extorting a trip
to 4A, the Psychoneurotic Ward (at
last!). By the Seconal-hazy, placid
end of that night, after I stripped
and was given blue pajamas and a box
of Kleenex, when I shuffled off
in canvas slippers to the john

and gazed alone into the mirror, I
had a smile, relieved I would never
be caught, knowing something was over
that could not happen again: I was
done with one "adventure" (if that's
what it was, that hidden life, the free
spontaneous days when the future
paused—nothing directly ahead except
imprisonment—and there was great, wild
love in the Bay, destined not to fail,
etc., but of course we couldn't help
that), and here was something new already
passing. I was smiling anyway, not crying
then or much at first for the gorgeous
weight of my unexpected stories (only
later discovering a lot of whatever
hadn't been cried for)—and don't yet
believe I've been punished "enough."

The 4A Shuffle

January to May 1970

Except for basketball or swimming, sleep
or showers, our white cotton
canvas-soled slippers went everywhere,
and it doesn't bother me much
not to forget
how the slippers sounded,
down long fluorescent corridors
between walls that were half
ceramic-block, half apple-green plaster.

Our slippers whispered as if
they spoke for us,
for a while the only voice
we shared, whispered
because we were shuffling,
and we shuffled
because we were drugged,

Thorazine-fettered and moving
in columns or bunches but almost always
solo, and the corridors of Ireland
Army Hospital remain
lit-up but somber,
glowing at night like
feeble sunrise, days
like dusk.

• • •

(I've walked no further or

slower than on a January
Saturday, my mother
up to visit and seeing
me for the first time
in over a year
dragging toward her
down the busy ward
corridor—and I
afraid to be seen
by a watchful staff
moving like someone
healthy, and so
going slowly, each
step, each minute
I take to get there
like walking on her.)

• • •

The patient is a 22-year-old single man who sits anxiously at the edge of the chair in the interview situation. His posture is rather rigidly maintained, changing little during each session. His voice is shaky and at times he is on the verge of tears. He has much difficulty articulating what he wants to say. He often reacts slowly to questions and seems to be preoccupied with his own thought process. He is indecisive and confused over what he will do and expresses vague feelings of guilt. His associations are loosened and he shows some blocking. He is completely void of any sense of humor, he is essentially in a state of depressive withdrawal. He denies hallucinations. He admits poor appetite, he sleeps poorly, he admits some constipation, he cries at times. His affect is flat.

The patient is mentally competent for pay purposes in accordance with the criteria established by AR 37–104; he has the capacity to understand the nature of and cooperate in Physical Evaluation Board proceedings; and he is not considered to be dangerous to himself or to others at this time.

• • •

JANUARY cold, cold—the worst in years—and Nixon
turns 57 on my first full day in the Ward, followed
by Chiefs vs. Vikings in the Super Bowl. Elsewhere,
my kind, big father is adjusting to Tucson and a new
family under a sky I imagine open, stretched over
like blue drum-skin. I dream I'm a hunchback
singing in a voice I don't have. Later, Spiro Agnew
is menaced by a knife-wielding Balinese "bad spirit,"
all in fun, on the day the civil war ends in Biafra.
More snow, or rain changing to snow. *Hee-Haw* is
clearly the second most popular TV show after *Laugh-In*
on the 4th floor of Ireland Army Hospital at Fort Knox.
We have to bring in chairs from other rooms for the crowd.

• • •

It happened, Barton's
sure, because of his many
(two hundred?) acid trips.
19, he was on the firing range,
he explains, and prone
like the rest, all set
to fire—when trucks
and Jeeps flashed
into his sight, running
wild all over
everywhere, finally

toward *him.* So
he pitched away
the M14 and ran,
and all the sergeants
were very angry.

Consequently, tonight
when Barton appears
in the smoke-heavy
dayroom and proclaims
in Draculean tones
to the few still awake
or unstupefied
that a *bat* is actually
skittering up and down the arid
bored corridors of 4A,
no one—no
one—believes him until
a corpsman with a coat hanger
chases it down and
kills it. Some of us
study the crumpled
body in the waste can,
self-enshrouded.

• • •

In a folding chair pulled into the center
of the smaller, least-used dayroom is where
alcoholic "lifer" Sgt. Allen customarily
stations himself, leaning a haggard face

down toward a sheen of buffed linoleum
saying loudly to the floor, "Hey

will you bring me a carton of
Marlboros?" or "Buy me
a grilled cheese sandwich at the PX"
and "When are you coming? Huh?

When are you coming to see me?"
and things like that.

•

The corpsmen tell us not to obey
the burr-cut Major whose
malady is at least partly
a life of commands—being
wholly unable not to give them.
So he suffers here. Snaps out
orders. Patients go by or
stare, don't listen. Gonzalez
from New York says "Fuck off, Jack!"

•

The Colonel is very pleasant,
a failed suicide, a mellow
well-educated Finance
Officer. When they visit,
his quiet wife and daughter

bring a lot of snacks—rich,
made well—and they share.

• • •

Out of the stockade and things
we know nothing about—what
he was there for, what was done
and so on—Clark arrives.
                              The very
darkness of his hair, his mustache,
unoccupied dark eyes
seem at first like a kind of stage-
craft: Clark designed to
plague us most, to be here as an agent
of no hope, villain of gloom, and
worse—to walk and talk,
be impossible to ignore.

Every day, rocking from side to side,
he'll be standing in front of you
with no flicker of passion
in his face or voice, saying
"Hit me" or
"Kill me.
Would you kill me?

Throw me out the window."
That's how he darkens
so much.

Once on a snowy day
he was staring out into that
off-light, undressing in the cold
middle of the dayroom and remained
unmoving, pale and remote
in a nakedness we didn't
look at long or cover, leaving
him in "*his* trip," in a world

not ours and that's good,
leave him where it's almost
what we want—Clark
to be *gone,* frozen,
not a rocking
nightmare but here

he is again, just
for us, 4A.

• • •

This is the week, the Ward Activities, this is SOP:
We wake up in the darkness of 0550, called softly
over the intercom to line up for Medication ("Time
to get up, gentlemen, Medication, Medication time"),
and three days a week we change linen—if able by
ourselves to unfurl and tuck neatly the well-folded
medicinal sheets. Shave Call, 0615–0700, all shavers
electric of course. Then the Open Ward patients
line up and shuffle off to breakfast (0700–0730),
followed by Closed Ward patients with our escort
of white-clad corpsmen. The cafeteria is one great

glassy box of light and space and I love its openness,
the pretty good food. 0730–0800 we half-clean the ward,
stooping drowsily and without enthusiasm for the many
butts, trash under couches and so on, then the floor's
buffed every day but never by me—guys who like to buff
don't give it up. The OT room upstairs is next (0815–0915),
time for catnaps by patients on heavy dosage, 3-D Bingo,
cards, daily work at the loom by Winfield, weaving something
for his wife, and leather-work by St. Thomas & Bros. to, say,
Issac Hayes, while I'm wandering around, drawing or making
something odd with wood, copper, ceramic powder, glue,
or staring out through a long stretch of 8th-floor windows
at a wide horizon smeared with dawn and a thousand threads
of coal smoke from smokestacks like cannons aimed at the sky:
Fort Knox. Maybe I just lean on the sill and miss you.
Sometimes this is the best time of day, the best place
to be. So back we go, to nothing scheduled: slumping
is popular, the TV running, some play rummy or knock
Ping-Pong balls back and forth, I write letters and
mope. Soon we'll have Group Therapy to fill this slot,
they tell us. We hope not. Medication again, just before
noon. Lunch. And then at 1300 we cross a field to the Field-
house, if it's cold or drizzly we go in shabby jackets, massing
first in squares filling elevators, stringing out downstairs
like a drill sergeant's nightmare of a column, it's wild,
it's great not to march, not to salute—madmen have no
officers—and Robert's tape-player might rock the halls.
The air! Even hard rains and icy breezes feel good,
spring could kill me. For now I feel lucky I can play
basketball in pajamas, lucky I don't sag like laundry in
steam on the bench by the hot indoor pool, tranqued-out.
Then we have another long late afternoon back in the ward,

droning meekly toward supper, 1730–1800. Medication after.
The nights tend to be a much longer story—another time.
Shower call. Medication call. 2200, Lights Out.

• • •

In FEBRUARY, out in the world, cold around Louisville.
Tricia, recently ill with flu *and* measles, feels
better, says the President. "Disorders" in Chicago
were meant to be "the first battle in a war," says the
prosecutor. Two long-time friends disembark in Saigon
with the Pentagon saying the percentage of draftee combat
deaths in Vietnam may be high but it's "no policy." I say
why not go to the Kenwood Drive-In to the "pot show":
"5 Flicks that will Blow Your Mind" (in order)—*The Trip,
Psych-Out, MaryJane, Riot on Sunset Strip,* and, till
dawn, *Hallucination Generation.* You can fire up in-car
heaters and later lurch out into the cold darkness of
A.M. to steal tires off school buses to stop busing,
as Lester Maddox urges. Or we can watch Lee J. Cobb
as King Lear on *The Dean Martin Show.* Your choice.

• • •

Squat Sergeant De Leon, Wardmaster,
strides into the quiet Utility Room
to inspect his beloved aquarium,
safe here from the dayroom's careless or
spiteful cigarette butts. "Here is one

dead." He murmurs alarm. "Let me see . . ."
Virgil and I, snacking,

watch while he scoops out a floating
guppie, lays it gently on the counter,
bending down over it (his glasses
slide, his scalp is shiny)
and then very gently

pressing a few times
till it wriggles, at which point
he returns it to the water,
swimming.
            He nods at us, says
"How you like that? You feed them?"
to Virgil, who did, so De Leon
grunts "Good" and flicks my hair
as he leaves. "You need a haircut,
Howuh. Get it cut
pretty soon."

•

Virgil and I eat chocolate snack cake
donated by the Red Cross
as we lean against the small fridge
and talk. "Do you like
this cake?" he says.

I consider it. "No, not really,"
even though I like chocolate.

Virgil chews, looks thoughtful.
"Neither do I," he says, adding

with true seriousness,

"But I like to eat it."

•

Inside the glassed-in
cubicle of the Nurses Station,
from which only the most muffled
sounds emerge,
                    gesticulating for blond
and rosy but severe Lieutenant
Novak, Head Nurse, swarthy De Leon
and a couple of corpsmen,
                                    Doctor Cuesta
delivers his account of a session
with Virgil, pointing our way,

while Virgil tells me, as we watch
the pantomime, "He said
you ever hear any voices? And I said, well,

yeah, ever time somebody speaks to me."
And everybody knows
Virgil isn't joking.

•

Winfield tells me Virgil is a multi-
millionaire! Or could be
if his sisters don't take away
his share in family coal-mining money

because, over Christmas,

at home on a weekend pass from Advanced
Infantry Training, Winfield tells me,
Virgil went out into the woods
and rigged his .22 rifle to a tree

to fire at and kill
himself, but
missed by two inches,
and wound up here.

•

"I want to tell you somethin'
but I'm afraid you'll laugh at me.
It's somethin'
I'm afraid of."
(What?)

"You'll laugh."
I smile.
"Promise you won't laugh?"
(Sure.)
"You'll laugh, I know you will.
Promise you won't."
I promise, but mention
how he sets me up for it.

"All right." He pauses. Inhales.
"Do you know what I'm afraid
I might die from?"
He snickers. "You'll laugh,

it sounds crazy." (Well,
what?)
"I'm afraid I'm gonna die from"—he

snorts—"LOCKED
BILES!"
I laugh. He laughs too.
All around his small,
oddly pinched-up-by-
laughter nose, little white spots
appear, as usual whenever
he laughs hard. He reddens, "No,
really," almost sweating.
We laugh on.

• • •

Jittery Red Cross Candy Stripers
push a rattling cart bringing
doughnuts and punch every Saturday
night into the dayroom "Here
you are!" they say brightly "Any
seconds?" And when I return
they giggle
"Oh he wants seconds," amused
that I—an *it*—could know I want
anything

• • •

There are women

for fat Dooley humping his pillow
night after night, no matter

how his roommates mock him

otherwise on these drugs
we're sexless
as blighted angels, smoking cigarettes
to the butt, not feeling the heat
yellow our numbed fingers

or maybe we're more like fixed dogs
sometimes ravenous for what
we no longer seem to understand

so the women who visit and the women
who work here—friendly relaxed

sisters, gentle daughters, bawdy
NCO Wives (all German) who come to play
Bingo on Wednesday nights, even
Lieutenant Novak whose high white scarf
Gonzalez publicized one morning, and she
blushed for her detected hickey—

burnish the haze of we who wear
nothing under quiet pajamas

• • •

In the ninth month of my AWOL days

on a Saturday morning in June, I was astonished
to be snug in a patio armchair at Nepenthé,

near Big Sur, gazing into an open fire-pit
as I held one hand of a woman born
on the island of Fayal in the mystical
faraway Azores, a woman stared at
for the beauty of a Portuguese Jewish Indian
Gemini face. I mean,
I was astonished to be me and be there.

(Shy and awkward in daylight,
we didn't know each other very well.

Nella. She was 30.) Suddenly
a pediatrician

and a younger friend who refused to open
his eyes at any time ("I'm

on a blindness trip")
imposed on our happy discomfort,
introducing themselves, the doctor

grabbed my free hand and pinched down
one fingernail. "Look at that,"
he scolded. "No blood.

No blood under the nail.
I thought you looked too pale,
have you been ill?" But

by then he was closer to Nella,

leaning in to that face. "So tan,

you look so tan," he cooed.

My mind went away. I left Nella
—gracious in talk, adroit—
to entertain and shoo these guys
alone, but I could tell she felt

how I stared at her.

> *Every day I make myself*
> *out of paper, ink, or I make*
> *what I hope for, every day*
> *I sit at the same table,*
> *I make and re-make what I hope*
> *for me and you.*
> *Then I mail it, or*
> *Virgil does.*

After the FBI had missed my visit to Palo Alto by only
an hour, I'd fled a berth with Kentucky friends who
had to be next on the FBI's list of names to check
and I sheltered a few doors up Judah Street with three
sympathetic women from San Francisco State, all smiling
Friday when Nella came by to drive me across the Bay
to her house in East Oakland, for a long weekend
babysitting her kids—a safe job. (She wanted a dawn
start for Santa Cruz, Saturday.) She knew I needed
money, couldn't risk work, and mutual friends told her

I was "good with kids." So Friday night I met
again her two boys and a girl and we played until
their bedtime, late, then I followed Nella

in to a lavender bedroom and we perched on the bed.
For its headboard the bed had a quarter-moon mirror.
Nella wore a nightgown, violet, short, diaphanous.

We watched TV, smoked mild dope, drank Red Mountain.
I don't remember anything we said.
After a while we didn't say anything and I got up
and said Goodnight, and left,
closing the door. In the living room
I turned out the light and hit the couch.
I couldn't sleep. Nella
called out quietly a few minutes later, asking
if I was really that sleepy, and I wasn't.
I put on my glasses and returned.
I sat down on the bed and Nella sat up, and everything
was obvious at last even to me so we embraced.

At the back of her neck the hair was fine and soft
and very familiar. We were trembling,
awake all night.

> *I like your hair frizzed-out that way,*
> *flicked with odd hints of purple.*

Before the kids awoke for cartoons, I got up
to go sleep on the couch for a couple of hours.
Later Nella telephoned her mother and they fought

loudly in Portuguese, but her mother took the kids
for the weekend. Massive clouds

lowered on the coast, moving in from the sea.
They thickened the fog blocking the sun.
When we reached Big Sur we stopped for Irish coffee
at Nepenthé, an oceanside spot, sitting outside
among other morning customers, peaceably.
Ribbons of flame lived and died in an open fire-pit.
Nella took my hand, squeezed.
We looked at each other, lowered our heads shyly,
raised our heads in unison

and saw two men approaching, their skins
perfectly tan, their teeth perfectly white.

"Now you two look very interesting," one man said.
His glasses were tortoise-shell.
"You're so fair—pale,

actually. But you're so dark."

"Oh tell me what they look like,"
said his boyfriend, whose hair was a bubble,
whose eyes were shut.

> *I see you standing up*
> *half-naked, dripping*
> *in that chilly creek,*
> *the rills, cascades.*

While I watched as she worked to free us,
the solid gray barrier of fog all around began to waver

and thin out, abruptly. With a glowing

diffuse and damp at first, a crescent moon
gleaming like an ornament

fixed itself directly, exactly above her head, and I know
I was visibly amazed, because she caught my rapt stare
and smiled quickly in a glance, averting hazel eyes.
Strands of dark hair lifted and shook gently
in a breeze full of salt. The moon

stayed embedded, the silvery moon-barque.
For the first time that morning I heard—I had been
transfixed all along—the Pacific, which
till then could've been a pond. Now

it broke into the power and sound
of a wave like a mountain rising to curl
over and I couldn't move, but it was 1969
and I didn't want to.

• • •

MARCH, march: 27 killed *not* in "combat" in Laos, says the
Trickster, but died instead in "hostile action." The next
day he and Ziegler explain further. A wave of bomb hoaxes
sweeps the country, mid-March, and Nixon and Agnew play
separate pianos at the Gridiron Club—Spiro pounding out
"Dixie" several times. My brother visits again, nervous
to be here, nervous with Virgil. And I recognize how I'm
living another definition of "normal." Another state of
emergency's decreed in Cambodia and NVA troops fire rockets
into Laos. More charged with murder at My Lai. NVA and VC

diplomats leave Phnom Penh. On Easter, Cardinal Cushing
urges amnesty for jailed war protesters, draft "deserters"
in Canada, and other "young dissenters in trouble." On Easter,
in Louisville, snow falls, and falls all the next day too.

· · ·

Standing in shade at the back of the Red Cross
lounge—the spring day
sunny, a breeze
rippling eight or nine pairs of blue
pajamas—my friend
Winfield (a counterfeit
schizophrenic) and I
share a joint with other patients, guys
from other wards, shot, torn, burnt, the more
honestly wounded than
Winfield and I.
                    The smoke matters less
than the act, to be out in such balmy
air in the middle of Fort Knox, breaking
several laws, feeling anti- or non-
military and other ways I can't
quite describe, except to say

how comfortable, how pleasant
to be with this group, on this day.

A distant Jeep backfires, loudly.
Winfield and I glance off at the road
then casually resume our talk but
turning back we see everyone else

just now getting up from the dirt,

dusting off, and we notice
how far away from them
we're actually standing.

• • •

A lot of eyes were like his, not crazed
but sunken, remote,
as if they were pulling back
into the skull to hide. I liked
Seales. 19 or 20, straight from Vietnam.
Afraid of ending up in a VA hospital.
One of those gray afternoons in February, March,
when the population of the ward
was low, and most guys were taking naps,
from the plastic couch in the dayroom
by the TV, Seales broke
my staring out the window, asking me
if I liked babies, "you know, nice little,
cute little babies?"
He was doodling in a *Life* magazine.
"You want to see some Vietnamese babies?"
And I went to him, knowing
from his tone that I didn't, and he showed me
a full-page photo of smiling fat quintuplets
with dozens of inked-in wounds.
It was worse because I wasn't surprised.

• • •

The son of a "full bird"
colonel, with orders in hand
for Vietnam, stopped off in

Cincinnati to use a medical library.
Then he went west to Louisville
and Fort Knox, to a hospital
room where he sat for days
alone and said nothing—for days
he sat and stared, and one day
the walls curled and were speaking.

(I tend to forget how the blue
eyes of bone-pale Winfield
darted most of the time, and how
much he blinked.)

• • •

On my first Sunday evening in 4A
I was drifting, tissue box
as usual tucked under one arm,
part calculated, part
practical for tearful
depression, simulated
or not. And in turning away
from Ed Sullivan on the dayroom
TV, I confronted a pair of dark
eyes locking onto mine, drawing near,
wire-rimmed eyes of a black guy my size.
His small neat Afro happened to be
back-lit and so
like a nimbus and he was smiling,
saying "Can I borrow one of your

napkins?" with a glee
barely stifled. I nodded—

I didn't say much then. He
plucked one with a stylized, dramatic
jab of arm and raptorial
hand, clearly meant for me to notice,

then quickly wadded the Kleenex
under his nose with exaggerated
snuffling—waiting to see
what I would do. I smiled,
faintly, which turned out to be

correct. This was self-named "Saint

Thomas" AKA Thomas Hudson, like me
a long-term AWOL but caught
at O'Hare, tripping.
                              Within a week
I and others see St. Thomas with an apple
in his hand and an earplug in his ear,
and a cord from the ear to the apple.
He's grinning a little with another
joke for us, the ward—a gift
from St. Thomas.
                              For the similarity
of the military fates we almost
share, and our birthdays
in April too, he defends me one day
to the Brothers
lined eight or nine in couches and chairs
in the narrow hall as I'm
passing by, mild, shuffling.
                              "Man,"
says Roberts, who is large and hates

many, glaring at me. "That guy
sure is a *dud.*"
                    "Yeah,"
says St. Thomas.
                        "But he's a hip dud."
I look back and nod once
dully, grateful.

• • •

Lantern-jawed
Virgil from Hazard
talks happily about his favorite sister,
oldest of four, and their game
on long summer afternoons in Kentucky
mountains: climbing

together into a big brushy pine
to lurk, waiting for a solitary
car to pass near—then sailing
a hubcap like a frisbee
down to the road for its
clangor and the smothered laughter

when the driver stopped and got out,
looking for something he hadn't lost.

• • •

President Nixon admires a proposal that psychological
tests be administered to every six-year-old to determine
potential for criminal behavior. Hundreds of bodies
of Annamite Vietnamese killed and dumped by Khmer Rouge

float down the Mekong River from Cambodia, and the stench
is profound. It's APRIL. Nixon announces troop withdrawals
and says he won't participate in the first Earth Day, but
will watch. On a Tuesday night, when an empty rocket casing
from Apollo 13 smashed into the moon and made a moonquake,
the moon "rang like a bell" for four hours.

• • •

I sleep facing left
because the gray feet of my
roommate Koss are bare, cracked
and smelling dead, odor of death
covering my head like a bag.
His dirty hair rises like grass

and once I saw him led into
the shower stall, soap
placed in his hand, water
turned on for him, and I
came back by an hour later
to find him still that way.
Nothing works for him, no
drug, not shocks in ECT, not
the quiet fiancée whose
visits intrigue us—imagining
Koss with another life, when
he's "Billy" and loved
by someone very pretty and nice,
when he could do more than halt
until prodded, could
smile or talk or even
finish a cigarette. If

we could see anything
like that—ever—I swear
on his slow eyes, on the terrible
meekness, all our steps
would lighten awhile
and for days, a *month,* our common air
might flower.

• • •

(I said goodbye to Winfield in the rain,
in fact, and stood outside Medical Holding
Co. barracks where I lived until my paper-
work cleared and I could leave for Oakland,
done with all this. And Winfield was going
back to New Hampshire, I think, on this day,
back to the wife who looked like a sister,
who visited and played Milles Bornes with us.
He was crying because some old pal of his
father's, another colonel, had wanted him
to drop by for a visit, and Winfield planned
to leave that day and would miss his flight.
He got out of it finally, but the last-minute
stress made him cry. He was still crying
a little when he got into the taxi in the rain.
He wrote to me once while I lived in Oakland.

(I ran into St. Thomas on my way to Supply
to pick up a field jacket. Earlier that day,
he said, he "fired on" a couple of Spec. 5s
from SPD—the quasi-stockade where he went
after his court-martial, before his discharge

—because they insisted that his Afro be cut.
He described the struggle, the rolling downhill,
punches, defeat. But he was happy he'd fought.
We shook hands and knew that was all and it was
good enough then. He went home to Chicago.

(I can't remember what happened to Virgil or
whether I said goodbye or not, whether he was
still there or not. I don't know why I can't.
I can see him by the card table in the Red Cross
lounge waiting for an invitation from Winfield
or me to sit and join us, and it doesn't come,
but he stands there for a long time anyway.)

• • •

I can close my eyes and walk down that hall again, all the way
from the locked double-doors to the dead-end wall of Closed Ward.
The odor throughout is constant, "institutional." Add the smell
of yellow-stained fingertips, amber liquid soap, acrid pajamas,
furtive marijuana in the officers' bathroom, roommates, smoke
—always smoke. It was part of the stink of a lassitude without
pleasure. And I can see again the ones who were most spectral,
like Poynter explaining calmly how his heavy arms got a bright
pink cross-hatch of scars, miming how he held the razor-blade
and used it so eagerly. Or that huge anonymous one of the many
quickly here, quickly gone, with a fist-sized dent in his skull
hurting his brain, making him helplessly fierce—who scared all:
a big new fish dropped at night into a murky aquarium world: I
awoke from a light dose of Thorazine and Stelazine as he pounded
the door in Seclusion, and nobody the next day could shrug off
how he yelled "Doctor! Doctor! I want to *talk* to you"—and that

"talk" inflected with death, and his eyes when he was leaving
glinted with hopeless unending rage: another public nightmare
but at least transient and not permanent like Koss or Clark, like
Johnson who arrived and went loudly from one patient to the next:
"I-I-I-I'm the one, I-I-I runned off, I left Fire Guard, I runned
off, it was me, I-I-I—" and so on, all around the dayroom, twice,
on a cold January night (he was very bundled-up). Someone said
MPs had chased him to the top of a water tower. He never improved.
Tried to drink from a 5-gallon drum of floor wax during clean-up,
so Cuesta sent him to Seclusion and his piss streamed out into
the hall, days later he shit in the hall near the room I shared
with Koss and—first—Collins who slept in sunglasses buried under
covers and one day threw a punch at Lt. Novak and then hit De Leon
and disappeared, transferred to the guarded 9th floor, then came
grim and manic Hazelet—and who? Maybe Elrod the Georgia farmboy
who rolled in one night on a gurney, the next day in fresh pajamas
sat cross-legged on the floor of our room in front of the beds,
a puddle spread out around him and his pants stained with something
not piss: I noticed empty aftershave bottles nearby as he was asking
in the thickest red-clay accent I've ever heard if I had a match.
And I felt a monk in an orange robe in lonely space, but my fingers
had already touched the matchbook in my pocket before I said No
and fetched a corpsman, whose thanks for what I thought no choice
made me remember how we were scolded when Clark stripped in the
dayroom and we ignored him.

                                   Sometimes I think about standing
in a groggy morning line, one cup for pills, one for water. Then
they would shine a flashlight into the mouth, under the tongue,
into the throat. Otherwise we liked to spit out the pills whenever

able, coloring urinals with streamers of dye as the pills dissolved.
But we couldn't spit out enough.

> (I know I was lucky anyway,
> and I'm not ashamed.)

If
in this place there was too much no one ever knew, and no
measure of care did anything to redeem fully
the ones who could stand quietly in the hall and trash your heart,
the ones lapping blood with a glance, the ones
who came and went,
who stayed too long,
then
      for the mercy of what we had
despite all that,
            I'm grateful—
for our brotherhood from a company of the fierce,
the mute and the buried. Because

Clark is coming toward me down the hall
in the hat and coat that he or someone lifted from Cuesta's rack,
and he's smiling, saying "Shake!"—hand extended.
                        It wasn't a lot,
but the patients had done it, we had done it
in our hatred of his scary distance and so
adopted and led him around by the hand. Without
that, no smile would be there. After,

nobody seemed as black or white to me, in any way.
No one would enter the Ward and turn invisible. No one

dragged down the hallway solitary, untended. It happened. So

the springtime sun becomes
Clark smiling and the sun on the hospital roof where we play
volleyball and burn happily to a Thorazine-aided ruddiness. People
fatten. It wasn't *thriving* but it was the best we could do.

That it happened
is good to know.
To tell it is another part of fortune.

> *Again*
> Seales and his buddy Franklin
> start a chant, it's too
> familiar, it's high school
> and maybe too corny but
> the sun is out
> and everything about the day
> lightens the gait of our column
> on the path to the fieldhouse,
> something feels just right about
> chanting "We are 4A,
> couldn't be prouder,
> if you can't hear us—"
> and so on for fifty yards.
> Only two voices,
> but they weren't chanting
> alone. I know
> there were more than three.

II. a landing

The Take-Off

I was belted-up inside an idling Delta turbo-prop
on a runway watching a shimmering jelly of humid heat
rise from asphalt and metal, when a dull brown
medium-sized moth settled astride a rivet on the silvery
stretch of wing between me and the cowling,
and clung there. Even after the propeller kicked on,
all it did was shift, aligning with the loud ferocious
wind, wings flattened. It stayed, still gripping
while we taxied. I leaned closer to the window
as we started the sprint down the runway,
wondering how long it could manage to hold
(and why). Only at our fastest, only in the seconds
before lift-off did it release? tear loose?
and shoot back blink-fast in the wash of the prop
to a raggedy life or quick death, I don't know.
I care more about the fact of its tenacity,
how its fate became too certain for hope and yet
something like hope became everything it had.

For Susan

Are there some acres of terrain you remember
in detail—could say exactly how the mossy
boulders jut and tilt along a limestone
creekbed for a stream just deep enough
to be called one, cutting through fields left
fallow, its distance from a gate of weathered
slats a quarter mile or so—and yet
know you were never there? Again and again
I'm walking alone in waist-high grass
with a recurring pleasure even the bare sky
deepens, expecting all things about to be met
in my slow trek by the creek, so comfortable,
where every tree is lush and fine like elms
and wholly familiar . . . but nothing
I've seen in real daylight. I wonder
how many times I'll be a vague presence
owning whatever the dream has meant before
waking in bed with the whole scene playing on
gently, a little sadly—like moments
when I catch myself talking again
to a long-dead friend, Susan's face
placid and listening, when I ache
as I do for the smell of the dust
stirred up by my feet in that place
I've never been, its heat of unreal
sunshine on my unreal body, the perfect
calm. That it's *not* doesn't hurt much
but the pain is odd, distinct,
like agonies of a ghost—never
touching anything remembered, unable
to forget, being never and always
there for others in what might not

seem to us like perfect silence but is.
Still, when I'm idling in traffic or
in some way not quite present, I imagine
now and then a softening gaze, a murmur
of comfort when I say what I always say,
hoping, half-expecting again to be forgiven
—until the cars speed up and so
become necessarily real, and move on.

The Oncoming

It was the Civil War
we fantasized: the cloud-to-cloud
and cloud-to-ground lightning
as cannonades, bombardment, and we
leaned in gray by the spikes
of pickets, awaiting
the assault to follow, charged
like the summer air
by the killing and death we could know
over and over—boys
on a porch in a suburb, brothers
in blood and spirit, not
talking, just staring out
at the weather approaching, lives
still simple enough
to relish an imagined waste, never
troubled even when huddling
on the roof, waiting for the bolts
to scare us down. We couldn't
know how much our histories
would one day give us
too much of what the other
has too little of—I with my
time and travel and apparent
freedom, my brother
unmoving, bound to loving
children, wife, a home. We
couldn't know how the night's
mottled, fitful brilliance
would one day bind us
in moments we recollect
as wonderful—but fated,
like the silver shooting across

our quiet smiles, to be
effaced by the rain
we knew was coming finally
to end the battles, when general
weather settled in and we
left our play and slept
without thunder in murmurous
steady rainfall, our beds
and all the rest apart.

Whatever It Gives

After an overnight storm, ice
cloaks the open surfaces of everything
outdoors, including two of three
steps I walk down at seven
when my ride comes by—one step
dry, then I slam down hard
on the next, on my back.
But I get up unhurt because I fell
too fast to think.

●

Five days a week I wear the same
old clothes and never shave, learning
ancient secrets of invisibility—to be
dirtied by labor, for example.

●

One day I'm out on a huge flat roof doing
cornice work, kneeling, driving nails.
Some friends make up this crew. Here,
this high, we see the weather coming.
The entire sky is changing, temperature falls
forty degrees in fifteen minutes and everyone
stands excited, freezing, still.

●

It rains too hard to continue
so we truck off to the Paddock Club
for beer and bad food. Exiting at dusk,

wavering in the mist of a spring
fog, I sing out loud, walking
the few blocks home. White crowns,
snakeroot, nod in my uncut backyard.
Two dogs come charging out to greet me.

•

I'm walking up and down a hill one day
in cold yellow mud, carting
lumber on my left shoulder like a White
Mule: 44 waterlogged 15 ft. redwood 2 × 10s,
two at a trip (88 in the stack, three
packing). And then we build decks, drive
16s overhead for the rest of the day.
At home, settled neck-deep in the tub,
I find an apple-sized
bruise on my shoulder. I pick lint
from a blood-capped thumb,
both arms, both shoulders twitching,
stiffening,
these good days.

Denizens

By a dry swale across a meadow
of tussocks, a pastureland of bluegrass
and fescue—the Mental Hospital

For a week we've been vanishing
ghostly creatures in a bright pall of dust

there, wearing cheap snouts
to be able to breathe,
stuffing ears with foam cylinders

hoping to muffle a continuous
jackhammer hell
in a windowless 18 × 36 cooler with ceramic
block-wall echoes and a killing
floor of three-inch concrete
then tile, then ten more footlike
inches of concrete cured harder
every year of its 35 or so—
and everything has to go

So we like our short breaks

With sore hands, we wipe away
the pale mask of work

We move outside
and little clouds of dust move with us,

trailing to where we slump upright
in the breeze, the blue air
Today, from above, we hear

a noise, we look:

thirty feet high
along the ridge of the cafeteria
roof strides a bearded man, tall
and thin and wearing the state's pajamas

He stops and waves
We wave too

Last Break

We lounge in comfortable dry grass
among our tools, our plastic hats.
Our horizon is full of smokestacks,
rooftops low and darkening in late afternoon.
Our horizon is tan, smog-bleached.

But overhead it's all blue, we tilt our faces
back for the sunshine
and the press of the sky's belly.
Like a known body
whose touch our affections once
heated,
        the day as it dies
gives us the best of last warmth.

Unsettling the Farm

Over everything drift
clouds of stars, rivers of stars.
Its Halloween profile sharp
in a sky of indigo, the pale orange
crescent moon wanes above a forested
ridgeline cut deep and left high
by the Elkhorn. Barking, yapping,
DuAnne and Pea-Wit agitate the night
around the house, as if down the hill
other dogs are coursing the long
creek-hugging arm of fertile bottomland
under its slab of ground fog.
Awake, fretting again about his sheep,
the farmer gets up and stares into the dark.

At daylight, after coffee and cigarettes,
he trucks himself and the help
to plant-beds to pull up and bundle
green finger-thick tobacco
for setting in the nine harrowed acres.
As the Dodge bounces along
in dried ruts, the farmer
spots a collie, a ratty stray
running hell-bent, spooked
by the pickup clanking. So
the farmer brakes, gets out
and whistles, wishing
he had the rifle with him,
watching the collie disappear
where the field turns to nettles.
Then the workday begins, heats up
and goes on into sunset, the crew

pulling plants, setting plants,
the farmer brooding—tobacco, money,
rain, mold. Work done, his supper
down too fast, the farmer drops
off into sleep and might dream about
his fragile crop. In fog,
pursued, his sheep run
desperately.

Grace

Some of the teeth may be mine,
she believes, but doesn't remember.
They had rattled in an old soap box
so I opened it and found a lock
of blond hair, several ivory rings,
and a lot of baby teeth like wrinkled
kernels of white seed-corn.
I pick up Pawpaw's snakeskin
cigarette case just the right size
for deadly Camels, cedar-scented
too from thirty years in the chest
her mother's brother made. We handle
V-Mail, birthday cards, telegrams
announcing grandchildren—all things
my grandmother saves, apologizing for them.
I read labels aloud, I open labeled boxes.
All along the concrete floor run sinuous cracks,
and she recounts the times she and Gus
swept water into the drain. We circle
the basement while she talks about pieces of
furniture, boxes her children store there,
stopping to flick away cobweb, dust. Then
I cup her elbow and slowly we go back
upstairs where the radio and TV together
make a noise of music and crowds of people.
And when I turn at my car for a final
goodbye, I feel the wave becoming
something remembered before it happens.
I drive away without leaving.

The Creturely

In cool bordering shade
down where the creekbank untangles,

I'm crouching in low watercress and mint
while two bluejays screech

maniacally—sharp notes, like a beak.
And I'm startled by a sudden eye-level

sparkle, a twisting thread of light and there,
below, a spider dangles—small, white, very

delicate really. I reach out
and I pinch the strand and don't know

why. The spider drops into a quiet
pool, sinks in the clear water,

I lean closer. Weirdly, you could say
"casually," as if it belongs there,

and slowly, the spider walks around underwater.
But out from a gap, a hole in a rock, stepping

sideways comes a crawdad, its one-inch body
edging up to what makes this otherwise empty

pool a new world. Tense
in their miniature

hostility, both strangers
rear, combative, feinting—just

light touches, as if
novelty makes them wary. Then a pincer

jabs and the spider dodges but
I think it's dying anyway.

Its hairlike legs ripple
as it drowns,

crumpling, wilted. The crawdad
waits, hesitates then lugs the corpse

to a little rock-mouth of shadow.
With needles in my legs I stand up

muddled, and trudge off along the path
back to my car. I come upon

a plump snake curled in thick dust
where a limb of the creek has dried and pink

butterflies assemble for the buried water.
They look like nervous petals.

The snake looks like a copperhead.
Then I remember cattle grazing here

so before I think any longer
I'm killing that too,

pitching through heavy air
a broad flat chunk of limestone

turning slowly in flight to land
on edge, exactly bisecting

what proves to be a cow snake.
Slapping dust, each meaty half

flails, and I'm impressed
by the throw, its deadly perfection

—I could never do it any
better—and then I feel

ashamed, if too late and possibly
not enough.

Justice

I can't say he totters or staggers
but the gait's unstable, a touch
could make him lurch, since
when he walks his feet don't
rise much, toes bear the weight,
his heels cant forward and so
he does—knees bent. The large
blond head nods like a flower.
His cheap unbelted jeans slip
too low, riding where his small
butt starts and you can't not
notice, not see the dark indigo
patch, a stain of urine. A thin
arm flops as he moves, the hand
passive, unflexed. The other
hand plucks at his crotch
continually. No one really
likes to see him approach
but no one is afraid, even
smaller children hit Joshua
who can only accidentally
retaliate well enough to
hurt, to drive them away.
One day I yelled at another
neighborhood kid—punching,
kicking Joshua for fun. (He
doesn't ever remember my name
although we say Hi and talk, I
answer questions, sometimes wind up
scolding.) From the permanent gray
crescents under blue, droopy eyes,
profanity spasms and a clear urge
to hurt, I suspect his parents don't

like to see him either, that they
abuse him. One day Joshua is near,
outside, calling "Mister! Mister!
They're hitting me!"—and I know my
name is there, I'm nudging open a blind
to look out. But it's already over.

Leisure World Safeway at Night

There is food
in rolling silver
cages, garble of tuneless
piccolos of registers, carts
clashing, sliding one after
one inside another with steady
floods of elder voices like
a creek torn by rocks,
vexed and chopped but
always flowing on, such
a weltering noise where they
pause very long, fingering what
they want, don't want—stopping
anywhere—and their heads are pale,
often delicate, in regulated air
crowded with scents, shoulders
bowed as they offer faces
hiding much of everything
they were, clinging to a tint
in fragile hair sometimes, maybe
red, maybe the makeup's too heavy
or a gentleman is cussing
quietly in the cereal aisle,
a muted plaint by rote
by now, to no one here
where everyone goes hobbled
somehow except me and a few
others, this checker muttering
back to a sacker about being
"trapped" after glancing at her

line growing longer, assembly
of old eyes nested, opaque,
intent on what's ahead
as they face a wall of black
windows scrawled with light.

American Chameleon

1. The Case

The skies still change all day
                              or do not,
but nothing lately has felt the same.

Or like this. I apply
Neosporin once again to tiny
blisters, wash and dry. Go
shuffling out of a bachelor
apartment. Traverse
a shaggy semi-tropical backyard
heading for a 1970 Ford Country Squire
with a smashed-out tailgate where alley cats
enter for tussles, smelly

frenzies. Pause.
                 At the backyard gate,

I glance at many fingernail-sized leaves on a blighted
old fig tree, young leaves chartreuse
and furry, extruded from the stubs of gray twigs.

Impressed, I stop to look closely.
                                    So far,
everything is more or less familiar.

Then I step back and gaze up into ragged dark treetops and above,
rapt in a way peculiar to these days. In hazy
spring sky it's as if
                       another basic cloudform—
beautiful, odd—
                happened to appear,

like one more token of the new arrangement.

Louisiana azaleas beyond the gate

fire reds and whites all along the two-mile gravel length of alleyway.
So I stand there a moment, staring, fingering keys.

I open a big rusting door. Note
a staggered column of fire ants bustling,
bearing larvae, colonizing
where many leaves blew in and remained
and became mulch under the front seat.

I slam the door.
                    Cubes of glass
pop off to join
                    hundreds already arrayed,
all pressed into mud
                    like a mat of diamonds.

Now I turn the key and scratch off.
Pebbles and glass fly
                    skittering into weeds, dust

rises.

2. *The Commentary*

(On the boundary between yard and alley

on top of the cyclone fence,
a green anole

bobs up and down
in push-ups quick,
chameleonic.
                    It halts
over lozenges of steel
which are empty, or full of air.

It glitters as if perfectly made
as an object for the pleasure of looking at.

He signals to articulate
presence, from his throat distending
                              a half-disc of skin,
sunset red.
Then the membrane retracts,
disappearing entirely.
No other is near.

He blinks against a cloudy swirl of sunlit
dust the car kicked up.

His turreted eyes ringed with pale iridescent blue
swivel, blink.

Again his bright throatflap appears.
In a way it's funny
                    —that persistence,
how it yokes
lizard to another

utterance just as necessary,

if not as literally
flesh,

     making one creature

glorious in how it's tangible,

making the other grateful
even in solitude to puzzle over
               words like "redemption,"
over twinges
      of what begins to feel inescapably like something almost

nameable, call it

      "joy," or just enough
             like that.)

III. a romance

Wake of the Undiscovered

Expensive little jammed-together houses glow and sparkle
prettily like HO railroad
                  accessories, and people
inside glow too
in their living rooms, dens, kitchens
                      lit brightly,
often left uncurtained—the lives there
both sealed-off and open to all
passersby, like a zoo
of model Disney
             citizens, so comfortable, so
pure they'd never fear any eyes or any
censure such as mine
as we circle the Big and Little Islands of Balboa,
strolling, talking, bumping shoulders in the light-strewn
salty night.

•

The bay's stilled water peels back
from the square prow of the ferry,
adding an undertone of splashing
to chugging, to murmurs from the cars
being hauled over toward the Fun Zone's
fragmented merriment drifting—and then
there is our own current of talk
and our surrender to where it seems
to be bearing us, sitting close enough
for the timbre of our voices, excited
by the chill and how we're finding
each other, to pulse like the swells
further out and be felt all through us
as we head for a lace of neon and fancy

strings of bulbs decorating the edges
of the dark bowl of the sky, obscuring
the few stars not washed-out already
by the massed incandescence of the Basin.

•

(Plenty of sun more often than not would be flooding
the most casual place on this Orange County campus,
highlighting pleasantly funky Humanities students
at our otherwise too left-brained university
whenever I came blandly to the Coffee Counter,
smiling at you and Brenda because you smiled—
only later being told that both of you watched me,
noticing I usually sat by myself. So
one day when I approached, gray-hearted, cloudy
with melancholy, you asked me how I was
and I saw your concern, your sincerity, which
startled me enough to introduce myself.)

•

He remembers what it feels like
to feel like a comet.
He knows how it feels to be driving fast
alone, singing, living forever.
He remembers a lot of what it feels like
to be 21. He doesn't know
what it means that he's as old

as her father and mother.
He thinks about it.

•

"It's better to look good
than to feel good," says
your grandmother, and she
means it. You
have to live that.
You grow up in Corona del Mar,
Balboa, Newport, the family
sails its own boats, you had
a horse. When I met you your tan forehead
rose high, curving into the naturally
blond hair. Lately
your hair falls down, and you're
losing more. Rings of charcoal circle
irises of pale blue slate.
Around the pupils, flecks,
dark ochre—eyes much too
hard to look away from. Your nose
bends and I never ask you
why. Then
that mouth. But in the only photograph
of you as a child
I've seen, your face looks sad.
Gray half-moons under the eyes.
The mouth turned down,

something that endured. One afternoon
on campus, early in our time
together, you told me about your illness
and I can't forget
that with every gesture and note of grace,
of warmth in the way
you touch your friends,
I'm watching a gradual
dying, a suicide.
(And there is no mercy
in your daddy's arms.)

•

At our feet, the benthic macrofauna of the Southern
California Bight thrive mutely, each small pool
crusted with sessile barnacles, it's a barnacle
economy in fact, their passive clinging
habits like those of ebony mussels in mats
threaded to red algae, which means
being eaten sluggishly by snails and starfish
and volcano limpets while urchins graze
the algal pastures of blue-green, red, brown,
and hermit crabs toddle in assorted housing or
hunt for empty shells to preserve their lives
as anemones quietly waggle pale coelenterons
looking like the unearthly colored plastics
owned by children.

Some beach boulders pose like hills, others like
stelae. We sit near, on big separate ones.
Wet-suited snorkelers bob just outside
the surge channel. Seawater

and the effluence of oil field
brine, tanker and line ballast,
cooling and refinery waste, sublethal
concentrations of trace metals
and pathogenic coliform bacteria
surge. Almost iridescent greenish-
tan stipes of kelp, yellowed bladders
floating at one end, long blades flopping
at the other, twist when the surf rolls
and pile ashore in dark-knotted clumps
like the unending wreck of some great hut.
For us, none of this matters
in the spumey breeze, the sun-borne air.

Along the paved oceanside terrace of the crescent
bay of Laguna, it's easy to walk. Many people do,
on a day colder than expected, cloudless,
windy up there. Kids you like or don't,
the overweight, the homeless, people you recognize
and the men who stare, the charred basketball
players and girls in tangas—that beach scene
receded when we paced uphill, sometimes
holding hands, yours cold, mine not. Then

we went down the concrete stairway to the ocean,
clambered over pitted spines of rock and found
space for ourselves, by ourselves, by the tide pools.
We talked and kissed and were happy—intertidal.

•

When I first played the songs
she taped for my birthday

and meant to reveal to me
more about her, and us, I heard
—after the last note—a door
slam shut: a coincidence
turning coldly metaphorical
days later when we met again
and I stepped up close and saw
our negation in her eyes—a change
abrupt and left unexplained,
a sea-change with no warning
and I sank in it.

:a tale from the 38 songs:

She wants to travel light. (A belle, if she wore gloves
they'd be fingerless.) A wheel turns, it's a low ride,
a perfect stranger?

Steps out of the shade. The promises like mist-colored
mountains, and they burn to be not listening, not thinking,
not wanting anymore. Now they feel so "different."

Stretched across a grave, she wraps up in what will always be
around her. He asked for the truth and she told him, these
dangerous days. This time she won't speak first.

The knots that won't untie—what if he was. Half-harvested,
doing this, doing that, partners, they felt it. The Boys
make some noise for her, abide in every sacred place. In
twos. It's all right, she says. Take anything.

It's dark outside. A sensual world and the moments that will
never happen, picked up in the fog, reach out like a child.
(It couldn't be him, that picture.) Executed, he hangs on,

she hates to lose him. She prays that he'll stay away forever.
She wants him as a dream and his part is over, those moments.
But they didn't die. (Maybe it hadn't started yet.)

Where was his mind, what was he thinking? Always changing,
too far or too near, she shudders in a flood of red rain.
Facades, without a noise, slip away. Survival—who moved
that sign? Keep that song away from them.

> *So the present became*
> *a veiled goodbye not*
> *uttered, floating over*
> *what we'd discovered and still*
> *lingers, with only a dark*
> *strait between those places*
> *where we live separately—*
> *and which we learn to cross,*
> *to be friends at least, in time,*
> *and for the rest of what we have.*

Even you, the blind, take a chance. I could show you
in a word. Is it raining in New York? We can walk.
You know me. And now you're talking, and we remember
a thousand never-known faces. True to life.

IV. a covenant

Walking for Points

Kentucky tobacco fields are good for it,
Cornfields too—any field recently plowed
And rained on, preferably, and unplanted
Or else calf-high, or harvested. I walk
With my head down and maybe the sky's
Wide, mystical blue, the air frosty.
Even if it's shitty—drizzling, hot—
I don't like to stop looking for any
Glints, signs of chipping waste, chert
Bits and flecks scattered like seed,
On damp days shiny, on the others
Faintly punctuating the dust. Ideally
But rarely, points can lie out on dirt
Pedestals, though better-hidden ones
Multiply the fun of pacing furrows: I go
For several hours on a hillside curving
Down to the Elkhorn, hills of clouds
Scrolling in from the west, and away.
Alone or not, this walking is quiet,
Passing over campsites of Archaic to
Mississippian range, where "Amerindians"
Broke open cobbles, flaked cores,
Chipped points and knapped edges—and I
Love the ghostliness, a feeling of lost
Unhurried mornings in a peaceful place near
Never-cut groves of trees, stands of cane,
A creek stuffed with trout, bass, mussels,
The air an excitation of birds, the wind
Smelling like nothing to be afraid of.
It may sound and be too idyllic and still be
True momentarily, at least when I'm going along
At my best, which is not caring much, feeling
Not at all anxious to succeed, to discover

Anything, happy looking. Then sometimes
A murmur from the populated calm says
Focus *now* so I do (not *thinking*) and always
I find something, broken or whole—obsidian
Spear-head, jasper bird-point, microlithic
Knife—or unrecognizable at first, like
A dusty chunk, ochre and gray, becoming
A crude hand-ax fitted as perfectly
To my grip as if I'd made it back then
And left it for another me to find,
Or that scalloped chip of flint
In rose and aqua bands turning out to be
A scraper perfect for a finger and thumb—
But just debris until between them. These
Things I picked up not knowing what they were.

Kinds of Bodysurfing

When I thought I'd broken my back
and was lucky to escape
breaking my neck
in a rough low-tide, big-wave,
walled-up surf; when I popped out of a curl
and pitched headlong, airborne, landing
a lot sooner than I expected
underwater in the sand between
jetties at Newport, hitting on the left
side of my face; when the rest of me
came over, bent backward by the heavy water
as far as I could bend
until I was bent a little further,
and I was surprised, even angry
at how that hurt, and then
afraid: I had to think in that
dilating snap of time
of limbs I might not be feeling
as my mouth sprang open
and I heard the scream, felt
bubbles coming out.

The effect of the next few seconds
lasted beyond the several
minutes before I went back in
slowly, cautious but not
wanting to be afraid and lose
waiting in a glitter of sun
for another good set, or pulling for a crest,
being grateful for the better slides across a face
or rocketing down a tube, riding
whatever's offered by another great earthly
power that you love and which doesn't.

Modern Life in Louisiana

At last he realizes how he is in fact
losing, which occurs to him one Saturday
morning on a gritty bathroom floor
while he huddles by the sink crying,
unable to stop—a surprise
out of what he thought was just the usual nowhere.
Since among his virtues is a gift
for microscopic attention, he can't avoid
noticing how each teardrop forms a convex
meniscus glinting brightly and so
prismatic that he wipes his eyes
and winds up looking for the source of this
unexpected light's particular
angle, the same angle painting a blazing
polygon on the bathroom's tongue-in-groove.
So is the sky he faces in the window
only another way of saying blue
eyes or mood or soul? Does the solitary
gnarled fig tree out back still utter
new leaves like an anthem of endurance,
or the single mimosa bend and arc
to press against the glass its soft-haired
flowers like a delicate private
passion? Or is it simply too many years
of celibacy turning everything
figurative? Maybe. Maybe
there's a kind of continuity after all
in ever-diminished expectation, as he begins
to suspect he knows what matters most
(at least temporarily) while the humid air
swells with a scented warmth, insinuates
with the same embodied handlike caress
that drove him to the floor. But

now he stands up and lets the air begin
to clothe him as if for another, that other
whose absence feels solid—like flesh,
like his own draped in sunlight—
and then the sunlight feels like a body
inside, where the comfort is enough
for a current of hope until he meets
himself smiling in the mirror, a tide
irresistible, a Mississippi.

On Earth, as It Is

He would look in her eyes one at a time, wherever they make their own
country, the best kind.
                              If she were here—those pale blue warrior's
eyes on his, her face rosy, very
                              Anglo-Saxon, British lips
forming British sounds, BBC
                              sighs—then

his contentment wouldn't be merely gazing alone into a shadowy backyard
    overgrown
with locust saplings and grasses harboring small animals in the heart of
    the city.

Now he thinks about another dusk, another
hot night two weeks ago in June, in the same house, in bed,
                                                  resting . . .

when a loud sudden chirr erupts from a big cicada next to the window
and she springs up naked from sweat-cooled sheets exclaiming

"Oh dear!" (There is
                  no such bug in England, no nocturnal insect ruckus
that loud.)
            For fun he alludes to what might surprise them in the Gorge
tomorrow—
            the infamous flying leech. And
                                          she believes him.
Never before and rarely again
                        has anyone succumbed utterly to one of his
meager whoppers.
                  But he confesses at once, eagerly (her trust
entire, so too

compelling). For his confession he exalts

himself, imagining
enlightenment, imagining
                    no more lies.

That variety of euphoria continues, as if viral.

The next day, each stretching a hand to the other high above
a creekbed after a snarled
                    rhododendron root
tore apart, they
                    titter together nervously
at similar ludicrous postures
                    despite the real chance of a mutual headlong
plunge twenty feet into a stone
                    chasm. Oddly, they remain
unafraid, and even his brother ventures a brief
                    chuckle. Soon

they're safe enough, after all, resting in the place they sought.
In a fog and unabating mist from the waterfall spattering in front of them,

they sit nipping bourbon while his brother wanders off examining
wildflowers, watercress, mint, ferns, lichen.

                    Rain begins.

Where a massive wall of maroon sandstone is scalloped, arching over,
    becoming
the lip of the falls forty feet above,

they shelter. They say nothing
for a while, in awe of the luck
                    of their bond, its
                              coincidence in time. So
he likes to be close to her. (Tonight

they're states apart. Telephone calls don't help, just muddle their unique
geography but they make them anyway, wind up
feeling that they could've been speaking in *Chorti.* Say
Goodnight. "I love you." Hang up.)

Absorbed by netted shadows of the locusts that canopy his brother's moonlit
    backyard,
he muses.
          Immersed in the comfort he perceives,
                                        as night and the simple
prehistoric leaves of the locust help unify his heart's disarray, he turns
to speak to the woman who isn't there—about sharing rooms
                                        serenely,
like colors both choose.
                    For a moment he stares at nothing.

Quietly he trudges through his brother's house
to the front of the house
to the porch, his brother, a beer, a joint.

Fireworks bloom and dissipate in glowing night sky
above an old stadium across a street named "The Avenue of Champions."
She won't
see that, won't hear
stadium-crowd exhalations waft past Burger King and float off

through haze suspended in the ripening trees of July or

hear the long whistling of burnt-out cannisters fluttering down.

Cherry bombs pop, pop, a block away.
                                        Tires screech, an engine revs.
In leafy maples, streetside,
                                cicadas chirr. He recalls

a scroll of lush treelines along the Interstate shimmering, speeding away
like her,
                and now in distant Buffalo
                                                she hosts her first barbecue
anywhere, for friends
they shared when they lived there,
                                        friends imagined here.

In the stadium another rocket fires, charring
                                                unseen ground, soaring
to a gaudy destruction. Celebrants, drunk,
                                                hoot outside, heckle traffic.
Refocused, he calculates
                            it's a week since she'd stepped aboard the jet, waving.

He'd driven home alone to this eroded plateau where Lexington sprawls, but

a phantom appeared in the sky-blue Galaxie beside him—after
that long embrace
in a stifling geodesic dome in the Greater Cincinnati Airport, after
their sticky goodbye,
                        when she flew back to Buffalo,

Niagara Frontier.

When fireworks end, crowds break up;

                                  visitors depart and the household
settles,
going to bed.

                Humidity oppressing, he squirms and flops till he sweats
enough to cool the sheets. His heart

                        plods, and the stillness

lets him be borne away. *Once again,*

                            as if dying instead of receding,

their shared terrain
embraces him.

Dark flurries of birds hurtle up from dense thickets,
hardwoods and softwoods, kudzu. The oldest
strata in Kentucky glide by, slowly quelling everything about them
as they ride with his brother to the Red River Gorge,

                                    a saurian wilderness.

Among cliffs, streambeds, stone arches,
                          chance and necessity
animate all life, even
                plants in "mute and merciless
                          strife," affecting every
stone in its persistence
             to *be.*
               A few burnished

                                        golden roots like veins but
more than a yard wide, flat,
                        thicker than legs, snake down and across
a sheer ragged maroon rock-face near a waterfall the thickness of one person,
spraying and plummeting forty feet into a dell
where nothing human has disturbed anything

for a long time—which almost disturbs the humans
                                        who rest here
after their trek, drinking Silas Howe.

Quiet as Shawnee, quiet as Boone,
                        they stare into depths of shadows,

alert to an ancient weirdness.
                        But even here the great forest remains
potential,
always Ortega's
                "a little beyond where we are." So where they are is now
their settlement, their
                        country—as they say when they talk, subdued
voices mingling with other sound in the dell, in gloom that yields to their
    pleasure.
Now his brother strolls over to the sandy boulder where they sit drinking
and they chat about small odd plants, how well they grow here, until the
    darkening
reminds them to leave.

                The As light rainfall fades to mist
they hike back to the truck and drive away, falling mute
when they ride through acres of long solitary hills

like huge sarcophagi in the smoke-blue moon-tinted fog.

It continues to be late on the Fourth of July.
All are far from the place where no one abides,

                               the heart of the woods.

Asleep in his brother's house,

                   he finds a way to hover over skylines, hover

in mid-air

          over stonebound meadows, to join her in rising

as a pair

       above humus, where

                  histories subside.

In the arrangement of his dream is proof through a night that no flags are
    there,
or anywhere. Their country is calm, community

                          untroubled in sleep.

Meanwhile the crickets and cicadas persist, dogs without
leashes and cats both domestic and feral

                     wander, birds

                        idle or fly,

soil animals labor mysteriously in their hidden
habitats and scattered

              people shape days from their nights.

Lightning bugs too
whirl up from fescue and bluegrass, sparks merging with a wheeling forest of
    light,

of cloudlike masses of stars

                 forever immune to most hope or expectation.

In fact those stellar glades

                    harbor the magnetic darkness of our

complete extinction,

but do the sleepers need to worry?

Some would think they're safe.
                          Certainly they thrive when they awake
in their territory,
                    unaware of boundaries
at first.

        Only the unluckiest people never find such a place,
but few of those who do
                          can stay there. One day,
like natives, they will be forced to leave.
Or maybe they appear to choose
                          to move on, like
pioneers. Either way

                they can lose it.
                          And the pleasant garden, untended,

the bright glade wasted or abandoned, drowse in a teeming silence

until the next life, a tentative footfall . . .

(As for me, who knows most of the names, who

cherishes the lost and hurtful,

difficult faces

and the tangle of their provenance,

I like to think I'll find the narrow path
                                    to the grace of whatever

is in them
that will not die, one day

                    when I'm home.)